TO:

Ovie

Love,
Mrs. Genovese

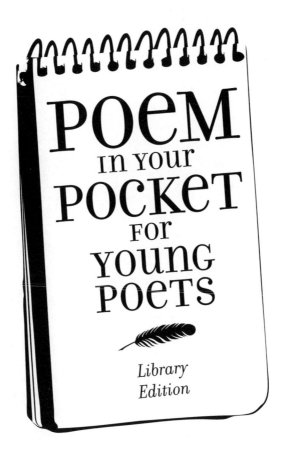

POEM
IN YOUR
POCKET
FOR
YOUNG
POETS

Library
Edition

PUBLISHED IN CONJUNCTION WITH
THE ACADEMY OF AMERICAN POETS

Selected by Bruno Navasky

AMULET BOOKS • NEW YORK

HOW
POETRY
comes
TO ME

How Poetry Comes to Me

It comes blundering over the
Boulders at night, it stays
Frightened outside the
Range of my campfire
I go to meet it at the
Edge of the light

Gary Snyder

Sunday

The mint bed is in
bloom: lavender haze
day. The grass is
more than green and
throws up sharp and
cutting lights to
slice through the
plane tree leaves. And
on the cloudless blue
I scribble your name.

James Schuyler

Substantial Planes

It doesn't
matter

to me
if

poems mean
nothing:

there's no
floor

to the
universe

and yet
one

walks the
floor.

A. R. Ammons

Eating Poetry

Ink runs from the corners of my mouth.
There is no happiness like mine.
I have been eating poetry.

The librarian does not believe what she sees.
Her eyes are sad
and she walks with her hands in her dress.

The poems are gone.
The light is dim.
The dogs are on the basement stairs and coming up.

Their eyeballs roll,
their blond legs burn like brush.
The poor librarian begins to stamp her feet and weep.
She does not understand.
When I get on my knees and lick her hand,
she screams.

I am a new man.
I snarl at her and bark.
I romp with joy in the bookish dark.

Mark Strand

The First Book

Open it.

Go ahead, it won't bite.
Well . . . maybe a little.

More a nip, like. A tingle.
It's pleasurable, really.

You see, it keeps on opening.
You may fall in.

Sure, it's hard to get started;
remember learning to use

knife and fork? Dig in:
You'll never reach bottom.

It's not like it's the end of the world—
just the world as you think

you know it.

Rita Dove

Permanently

One day the Nouns were clustered in the street.
An Adjective walked by, with her dark beauty.
The Nouns were struck, moved, changed.
The next day a Verb drove up, and created the Sentence.

Each Sentence says one thing—for example, "Although it was a
    dark rainy day when the Adjective walked by, I shall remember
    the pure and sweet expression on her face until the day I perish
    from the green, effective earth."
Or, "Will you please close the window, Andrew?"
Or, for example, "Thank you, the pink pot of flowers on the window
    sill has changed color recently to a light yellow, due to the heat
    from the boiler factory which exists nearby."

In the springtime the Sentences and the Nouns lay silently on the
    grass.
A lonely Conjunction here and there would call, "And! But!"
But the Adjective did not emerge.

As the adjective is lost in the sentence,
So I am lost in your eyes, ears, nose, and throat—
You have enchanted me with a single kiss
Which can never be undone
Until the destruction of language.

Kenneth Koch

Then and Now

THE RAIN

is speaking it pelts
against the windows
and on the roof
in the night
it makes thousands
of little words
which confuse the child
who does not understand
such a language
what is the rain
trying to tell him
should he be afraid
is there a message
of danger to be escaped
or can he be lulled
by the sound of the rain
and go back to sleep?

THE POEM

is moving by itself
it proceeds of its
own accord
the writer of the poem
has no idea where
it will lead him
he cannot control it
because it has
its own life
separate from his own
what if it carries him off
from his safe life
from his accustomed loves
should he fear harm
from the poem and tear up
the page or simply put it
aside and go back to sleep?

James Laughlin

To P. J. (2 yrs old who sed write a poem for me in Portland, Oregon)

if i cud ever write a
poem as beautiful as u
little 2/yr/old/brotha,
i wud laugh, jump, leap
up and touch the stars
cuz u be the poem i try for
each time i pick up a pen and paper.
u. and Morani and Mungu
be our blue/blk/stars that
will shine on our lives and
makes us finally BE.
if i cud ever write a poem as beautiful
as u, little 2/yr/old/brotha,
poetry wud go out of bizness.

Sonia Sanchez

The Dog of Art

That dog with daisies for eyes
who flashes forth
flame of his very self at every bark
is the Dog of Art.
Worked in wool, his blind eyes
look inward to caverns and jewels
which they see perfectly,
and his voice
measures forth the treasure
in music sharp and loud,
sharp and bright,
bright flaming barks,
and growling smoky soft, the Dog
of Art turns to the world
the quietness of his eyes.

Denise Levertov

FROM *Leaves of Grass*

The words of the true poems give you more than poems,
They give you to form for yourself poems, religions, politics, war,
    peace, behavior, histories, essays, daily life, and every thing
    else,
They balance ranks, colors, races, creeds, and the sexes,
They do not seek beauty, they are sought,
Forever touching them or close upon them follows beauty, longing,
    fain, love-sick.

They prepare for death, yet they are not the finish, but rather the
    outset,
They bring none to his or her terminus or to be content and full,
Whom they take they take into space to behold the birth of stars,
    to learn one of the meanings,
To launch off with absolute faith, to sweep through the ceaseless
    rings and never be quiet again.

Walt Whitman

THE
SWEET
EARTH

Storm Ending

Thunder blossoms gorgeously above our heads
Great, hollow, bell-like flowers,
Rumbling in the wind,
Stretching clappers to strike our ears . .
Full-lipped flowers
Bitten by the sun
Bleeding rain
Dripping rain like golden honey—
And the sweet earth flying from the thunder.

Jean Toomer

The Outlet

My river runs to thee:
Blue sea, wilt welcome me?

My river waits reply.
Oh sea, look graciously!

I'll fetch thee brooks
From spotted nooks,—

Say, sea,
Take me!

Emily Dickinson

The Pasture

I'm going out to clean the pasture spring;
I'll only stop to rake the leaves away
(And wait to watch the water clear, I may):
I sha'n't be gone long.—You come too.

I'm going out to fetch the little calf
That's standing by the mother. It's so young,
It totters when she licks it with her tongue.
I sha'n't be gone long.—You come too.

Robert Frost

the detail

on the rock overlooking the huddled rock-gorge
on the rock planted on rock for a wall
on the rock rusted with a rosy haze in it
on the rock children scrawl with chalk
    as though that were a way of making it talk
you can see circling about with a crazy velocity
as if the grain of the rock were reassembling
    for some unforeseeable purpose
red specks that are the tiniest spiders
             if you look real close

Cid Corman

maggie and milly and molly and may

maggie and milly and molly and may
went down to the beach(to play one day)

and maggie discovered a shell that sang
so sweetly she couldn't remember her troubles,and

milly befriended a stranded star
whose rays five languid fingers were;

and molly was chased by a horrible thing
which raced sideways while blowing bubbles:and

may came home with a smooth round stone
as small as a world and as large as alone.

For whatever we lose(like a you or a me)
it's always ourselves we find in the sea

e. e. cummings

Solitude

There now, where the first crumb
Falls from the table
You think no one hears it
As it hits the floor

But somewhere already
The ants are putting on
Their Quakers' hats
And setting out to visit you.

Charles Simic

The Brave Man

The sun, that brave man,
Comes through boughs that lie in wait,
That brave man.

Green and gloomy eyes
In dark forms of the grass
Run away.

The good stars,
Pale helms and spiky spurs,
Run away.

Fears of my bed,
Fears of life and fears of death,
Run away.

That brave man comes up
From below and walks without meditation,
That brave man.

Wallace Stevens

Fall

No, no, no, the leaves are saying, thrashing about in the wind.
We don't want to go; we don't want to be parted from our branch.
We love it here, even as we brown with age. Love must be forever,
or it is not love, and the leaves fling themselves to and fro in
the wind. The dark comes and no longer can the leaves be seen,
though they can be heard thrashing to and fro and against each other.

David Ignatow

Revival

Snow is a mind
falling, a continuous breath
of climbs, loops, spirals,
dips into the earth
like white fireflies
wanting to land, finding
a wind between houses,
diving like moths
into their own light
so that one wonders
if snow is a wing's
long memory across winter.

Steve Crow

The Waking

I strolled across
An open field;
The sun was out;
Heat was happy.

This way! This way!
The wren's throat shimmered,
Either to other,
The blossoms sang.

The stones sang,
The little ones did,
And flowers jumped
Like small goats.

A ragged fringe
Of daisies waved;
I wasn't alone
In a grove of apples.

Far in the wood
A nestling sighed;
The dew loosened
Its morning smells.

I came where the river
Ran over stones:
My ears knew
An early joy.

And all the waters
Of all the streams
Sang in my veins
That summer day.

Theodore Roethke

LOTS
OF
PLAY

Lots of Play

Lots of play

in the way things work,
in the way things are.

History is made of mistakes.

yet—on the surface—
the world looks OK

lots of play.

Gary Snyder

At the Playground

Away down deep and away up high,
a swing drops you into the sky.
Back, it draws you away down deep,
forth, it flings you in a sweep
all the way to the stars and back
—Goodby, Jill; Goodby, Jack:
shuddering climb wild and steep,
away up high, away down deep.

William Stafford

The Mind Dances

The mind dances
           when the body lets it

And when the body cannot
             the mind dances within

But sometimes they move together
                 and together sway
              and fly together
                  and dance and sing

And then it is indeed
            an enchanting thing

Lawrence Ferlinghetti

Seesaw

SONG

Days are bright,
Nights are dark.
We play seesaw
In the park.

Look at me
And my friend
Freckleface
The other end.

Shiny board
Between my legs.
Feet crunch down
On the twigs.

I crouch close
To the ground
Till it's time:
Up I bound.

Legs go loose,
Legs go tight.
I drop down
Like the night.

Like a scales.
Give and take,
Take and give
My legs ache.

So it ends
As it begins.
Off we climb
And no one wins.

Thom Gunn

Instruction

The coach has taught her how to swing,
run bases, slide, how to throw
to second, flip off her mask for fouls.

Now, on her own, she studies
how to knock the dirt out of her cleats,
hitch up her pants, miss her shoulder
with a stream of spit, bump
her fist into her catcher's mitt,
and stare incredulously at the ump.

Conrad Hilberry

Analysis of Baseball

It's about
the ball,
the bat,
and the mitt.
Ball hits
bat, or it
hits mitt.
Bat doesn't
hit ball, bat
meets it.
Ball bounces
off bat, flies
air, or thuds
ground (dud)
or it
fits mitt.

Bat waits
for ball
to mate.
Ball hates
to take bat's
bait. Ball
flirts, bat's
late, don't
keep the date.
Ball goes in
(thwack) to mitt,
and goes out
(thwack) back
to mitt.

Ball fits
mitt, but
not all
the time.
Sometimes
ball gets hit
(pow) when bat
meets it,
and sails
to a place
where mitt
has to quit
in disgrace.
That's about
the bases
loaded,
about 40,000
fans exploded.

It's about
the ball,
the bat,
the mitt,
the bases
and the fans.
It's done
on a diamond,
and for fun.
It's about
home, and it's
about run.

May Swenson

Afternoon on a Hill

I will be the gladdest thing
    Under the sun!
I will touch a hundred flowers
    And not pick one.

I will look at cliffs and clouds
    With quiet eyes,
Watch the wind bow down the grass,
    And the grass rise.

And when lights begin to show
    Up from the town,
I will mark which must be mine,
    And then start down!

Edna St. Vincent Millay

Makin' Jump Shots

He waltzes into the lane
`cross the free-throw line,
fakes a drive, pivots,
floats from the asphalt turf
in an arc of black light,
and sinks two into the chains.

One on one he fakes
down the main, passes
into the free lane
and hits the chains.

A sniff in the fallen air—
he stuffs it through the chains
riding high:
"traveling" someone calls—
and he laughs, stepping
to a silent beat, gliding
as he sinks two into the chains.

Michael S. Harper

Hide and Seek

It's hard not
to jump out
instead of
waiting to be
found. It's
hard to be
alone so long
and then hear
someone come
around. It's
like some form
of skin's developed
in the air
that, rather
than have torn,
you tear.

Kay Ryan

Primer

This kid got so dirty
Playing in the ashes

When they called him home,
When they yelled his name over the ashes,

It was a lump of ashes
That answered.

Little lump of ashes, they said,
Here's another lump of ashes for dinner,

To make you sleepy,
And make you grow strong.

Charles Simic

PUPPIES
OF
HUSH

Summer's Bounty

berries of Straw
berries of Goose
berries of Huckle
berries of Dew

berries of Boisen
berries of Black
berries of Rasp
berries of Blue

berries of Mul
berries of Cran
berries of Elder
berries of Haw

apples of Crab
apples of May
apples of Pine
apples of Love

nuts of Pea
nuts of Wal
nuts of Hazel
nuts of Chest

nuts of Brazil
nuts of Monkey
nuts of Pecan
nuts of Grape

beans of Lima
beans of French
beans of Coffee
beans of Black

beans of Jumping
beans of Jelly
beans of Green
beans of Soy

melons of Water
melons of Musk
cherries of Pie
cherries of Choke

glories of Morning
rooms of Mush
days of Dog
puppies of Hush

May Swenson

The Sniffle

In spite of her sniffle,
Isabel's chiffle.
Some girls with a sniffle
Would be weepy and tiffle;
They would look awful,
Like a rained-on waffle,
But Isabel's chiffle
In spite of her sniffle.
Her nose is more red
With a cold in her head,
But then, to be sure,
Her eyes are bluer.
Some girls with a snuffle,
Their tempers are uffle,
But when Isabel's snivelly
She's snivelly civilly,
And when she is snuffly
She's perfectly luffly.

Ogden Nash

Eletelephony

Once there was an elephant,
Who tried to use the telephant—
No! No! I mean an elephone
Who tried to use the telephone—
(Dear me! I am not certain quite
That even now I've got it right.)
Howe'er it was, he got his trunk
Entangled in the telephunk;
The more he tried to get it free,
The louder buzzed the telephee—
(I fear I'd better drop the song
Of elephop and telephong!)

Laura E. Richards

Teleology

Some things
are so

big that
it's hard

to tell
you're going

round going
round them.

A. R. Ammons

A Very Valentine

Very fine is my valentine.
Very fine and very mine.
Very mine is my valentine very mine and very fine.
Very fine is my valentine and mine, very fine very mine and mine is
    my valentine.

Gertrude Stein

Home to Roost

The chickens
are circling and
blotting out the
day. The sun is
bright, but the
chickens are in
the way. Yes,
the sky is dark
with chickens,
dense with them.
They turn and
then they turn
again. These
are the chickens
you let loose
one at a time
and small—
various breeds.
Now they have
come home
to roost—all
the same kind
at the same speed.

Kay Ryan

the sky

```
                the sky
                was     can dy
        lu                  mi
                nous            ed
                                i
                ble
                    spry   pinks
                    shy          lem
                ons
                                        greens
        cool
       choco                   lates
                un                              der
    a      lo
           co
           mo                   tive              s pout
                            ing
                vi
         o                  lets
```

e. e. cummings

One Day

One day after another—
perfect.
They all fit.

Robert Creeley

Maudell's Moon

Moon on your back, where you get
that moon on your back?

She stops. She just stands
and don't pose. She don't know
how she got that moon on her back.
She did not know she got the moon
on her back. She turn around,
she don't see no moon on her back.
    You lyin'.

Moon back on your back how you get
that moon back on your back?

> *You got a parsnip? I'll trade you
> that moon for a parsnip.*

Deal.

She walk on. She ain't had no moon
at all, but she got something now.

Thylias Moss

Capacity

CAPACITY 26 PASSENGERS
—sign in a bus

Affable, bibulous,
corpulent, dull,
eager-to-find-a-seat,
formidable,
garrulous, humorous,
icy, jejune,
knockabout, laden-
with-luggage (maroon),
mild-mannered, narrow-necked,
oval-eyed, pert,
querulous, rakish,
seductive, tart, vert-
iginous, willowy,
xanthic (or yellow),
young, zebuesque are my
passengers fellow.

WHERE
YOU
NEVER
WERE

You travel a path on paper

You travel a path on paper
and discover you're in a city
you only thought about before.

It's a Sunday marketplace. Parakeets and finches
are placed on the stones
and poppies in transparent wrapping.

How can you be where you never were?
And how did you find the way—with your mind
your only measure?

Fanny Howe

Brontosaurus

I keep writing about dinosaurs.
They lumber across the planet,
swim in the warm currents of the sea
and play all afternoon.
They have to be home by five.
I miss them.

Kimiko Hahn

Earthy Anecdote

Every time the bucks went clattering
Over Oklahoma
A firecat bristled in the way.

Wherever they went,
They went clattering,
Until they swerved
In a swift, circular line
To the right,
Because of the firecat.

Or until they swerved
In a swift, circular line
To the left,
Because of the firecat.

The bucks clattered.
The firecat went leaping,
To the right, to the left,
And
Bristled in the way.

Later, the firecat closed his bright eyes
And slept.

Wallace Stevens

The Tree

I am four monkeys.
One hangs from a limb,
tail-wise,
chattering at the earth;
another is cramming his belly with cocoanut;
the third is up in the top branches,
quizzing the sky;
and the fourth—
he's chasing another monkey.
How many monkeys are you?

Alfred Kreymborg

Behind Stowe

I heard an elf go whistling by,
A whistle sleek as moonlit grass,
That drew me like a silver string
To where the dusty, pale moths fly,
And make a magic as they pass;
And there I heard a cricket sing.

His singing echoed through and through
The dark under a windy tree
Where glinted little insects' wings.
His singing split the sky in two.
The halves fell either side of me,
And I stood straight, bright with moon-rings.

Elizabeth Bishop

Fishmonger

I have taken scales from off
The cheeks of the moon.
I have made fins from bluejays' wings,
I have made eyes from damsons in the shadow.
I have taken flushes from the peachlips in the sun.
From all these I have made a fish of heaven for you,
Set it swimming on a young October sky.
I sit on the bank of the stream and watch
The grasses in amazement
As they turn to ashy gold.
Are the fishes from the rainbow
Still beautiful to you,
For whom they are made,
For whom I have set them,
Swimming?

Marsden Hartley

Dog

The sky is the belly of a large dog,
sleeping.
All day the small gray flag of his ear
is lowered and raised.
The dream he dreams has no beginning.

Here on earth we dream
a deep-eyed dog sleeps under our stairs
and will rise to meet us.
Dogs curl in dark places,
nests of rich leaves.
We want to bury ourselves
in someone else's home.

The dog who floats over us
has no master.
If there were people who loved him,
he remembers them equally,
the one who smelled like smoke,
the one who brought bones from the restaurant.
It is the long fence
of their hoping he would stay
that he has jumped.

Naomi Shihab Nye

The Lighted Window

A lighted window floats through the night like a piece of paper in the wind.

I want to see into it. I want to climb through into its lighted room.

As I reach for it it slips through the trees. As I chase it it rolls and tumbles into the air and skitters on through the night . . .

Russell Edson

The Trap

Inside the old chair
I found another chair;
though smaller, I liked
sitting in it better.
Inside that chair
I found another chair;
though smaller, in
many ways I felt
good sitting in it.
Inside that chair
I found another chair;
it was smaller and
seemed to be made
just for me.
Inside that chair,
still another;
it was very small,
so small I could
hardly get out of it.
Inside that chair
I found yet another;
and in that, another,
and another, until
I was sitting in
a chair so small
it would be difficult
to say I was sitting
in a chair at all.

I could not rise
or fall, and no one
could catch me.

James Tate

The Delight Song of Tsoai-talee

I am a feather on the bright sky
I am the blue horse that runs in the plain
I am the fish that rolls, shining, in the water
I am the shadow that follows a child
I am the evening light, the lustre of meadows
I am an eagle playing with the wind
I am a cluster of bright beads
I am the farthest star
I am the cold of the dawn
I am the roaring of the rain
I am the glitter on the crust of the snow
I am the long track of the moon in a lake
I am a flame of four colors
I am a deer standing away in the dusk
I am a field of sumac and the pomme blanche
I am an angle of geese in the winter sky
I am the hunger of a young wolf
I am the whole dream of these things
You see, I am alive, I am alive
I stand in good relation to the earth
I stand in good relation to the gods
I stand in good relation to all that is beautiful
I stand in good relation to the daughter of Tsen-tainte
You see, I am alive, I am alive

N. Scott Momaday

LITTLE
FISH

Little Fish

The tiny fish enjoy themselves
in the sea.
Quick little splinters of life,
their little lives are fun to them
in the sea.

D. H. Lawrence

Rain in Ohio

The robin cries: *rain!*
The crow calls: *plunder!*

The blacksnake climbing
in the vines halts
his long ladder of muscle

while the thunderheads whirl up
out of the white west,

their dark hooves nicking
the tall trees as they come.

Rain, rain, rain! sings the robin
frantically, then flies for cover.

The crow hunches.
The blacksnake

pours himself swift and heavy
into the ground.

Mary Oliver

The Panther

The panther is like a leopard,
Except it hasn't been peppered.
Should you behold a panther crouch,
Prepare to say Ouch.
Better yet, if called by a panther,
Don't anther.

Ogden Nash

Magic Words to Feel Better

INUIT SONG

SEA GULL
who flaps his wings
over my head
       in the blue air,

you GULL up there
dive down
       come here
take me with you
       in the air!

Wings flash by
my mind's eye
and I'm up there sailing
in the cool air,
       a-a-a-a-a-ah,
           in the air.

translated by Edward Field
after Nakasuk

The Sloth

In moving-slow he has no Peer.
You ask him something in his Ear,
He thinks about it for a Year;

And, then, before he says a Word
There, upside down (unlike a Bird),
He will assume that you have Heard—

A most Ex-as-per-at-ing Lug.
But should you call his manner Smug,
He'll sigh and give his Branch a Hug;

Then off again to Sleep he goes,
Still swaying gently by his Toes,
And you just *know* he knows he knows.

Theodore Roethke

A Jellyfish

Visible, invisible,
　　a fluctuating charm
an amber-tinctured amethyst
　　inhabits it, your arm
approaches and it opens
　　and it closes; you had meant
to catch it and it quivers;
　　you abandon your intent.

Moment

I saw a young deer standing
Among the languid ferns.
Suddenly he ran—
And his going was absolute,
Like the shattering of icicles
In the wind.

Hildegarde Flanner

The White Horse

The youth walks up to the white horse, to put its halter on
and the horse looks at him in silence.
They are so silent, they are in another world.

D. H. Lawrence

FROM She Had Some Horses

She had some horses.

She had horses who were bodies of sand.
She had horses who were maps drawn of blood.
She had horses who were skins of ocean water.
She had horses who were the blue air of sky.
She had horses who were fur and teeth.
She had horses who were clay and would break.
She had horses who were splintered red cliff.

She had some horses.

She had horses who danced in their mother's arms.
She had horses who thought they were the sun and their
bodies shone and burned like stars.
She had horses who waltzed nightly on the moon.
She had horses who were much too shy, and kept quiet
in stalls of their own making.

She had some horses.

She had horses who called themselves, "horse".
She had horses who called themselves, "spirit", and kept
their voices secret and to themselves.
She had horses who had no names.
She had horses who had books of names.

She had some horses.

She had some horses she loved.
She had some horses she hated.

These were the same horses.

Joy Harjo

Why Animals Stay Away

An owl landed in a tree
next to the house
and spoke to me
in its language
which is comforting
like the second language
of mothers who are divorced
and have children.
I called back to the owl
using its human name,
but it did not come.
I called it Carlos,
but nothing.
I tried to speak
its language, but I
could not. The distance
in between us
was a third animal.

Alberto Ríos

THE
WILD
CHEESE

The Wild Cheese

A head of cheese raised by wolves
or mushrooms
recently rolled into
the village, it
could neither talk nor
walk upright.

Small snarling boys ran
circles around it;
and just as they began
throwing stones, the Mayor
appeared and dispersed them.

He took the poor ignorant
head of cheese home,
and his wife scrubbed it
all afternoon before
cutting it with a knife
and serving it after dinner.

The guests were delighted
and exclaimed far into the night,
"That certainly was a wild cheese!"

James Tate

Maybe, Tomatoes

if the vines mature
if the caterpillars don't get them

if we water, sucker, feed
if we pick and preserve

maybe, tomatoes
   thin sliced on sandwiches
   chunked into salads
      peeled and whole
      juiced and sauced
        stewed
          pickled
            stuffed

Connie J. Green

The Hot Stove

Mother was like a juggler,
she could cook five things
at the same time, & if she made
a mistake, one dish was overcooked,
she wouldn't be deterred,
she would just balance it out,
serve something a little raw.

Hal Sirowitz

Still Life

FROM A POEM BY BUDDHADEVA BOSE

What *are* you, apple! There are men
Who, biting an apple, blind themselves to bowl, basket
Or whatever and in a strange spell feel themselves
Like you outdoors and make us wish
We too were in the sun and night alive with sap.

George Oppen

Mortal Combat

You can't tell yourself not to think
of the English muffin because that's what
you just did, and now the idea
of the English muffin has moved
to your salivary glands and caused
a ruckus. But I am more powerful
than you, salivary glands, stronger
than you, idea, and able to leap
over you, thoughts that keep coming
like an invading army trying to pull
me away from who I am. I am
a squinty old fool stooped over
his keyboard having an anxiety attack
over an English muffin! And
that's the way I like it.

Ron Padgett

This Is Just to Say

I have eaten
the plums
that were in
the icebox

and which
you were probably
saving
for breakfast

Forgive me
they were delicious
so sweet
and so cold

William Carlos Williams

FROM The Good Moolly Cow

Come! supper is ready;
    Come! boys and girls, now,
For here is fresh milk
    From the good moolly cow.

Have done with your fife,
    And your row de dow dow,
And taste this sweet milk
    From the good moolly cow.

When children are hungry,
    O, who can tell how
They love the fresh milk
    From the good moolly cow!

So, when you meet moolly,
    Just say, with a bow,
"Thank you for your milk,
    Mrs. Good Moolly Cow."

Eliza Lee Follen

Only Cherries?

They didn't want me around
Said I couldn't have no cherries
Or watch them pick cherries
Or even stand near the table
Where one of those Kultur-Kookie-Klucks
With the big fat-legged smile
Was fixing to pop a nice red cherry
In on top of his gold spoon
You know I don't like those people
Who act as if a cherry
Was something they'd personally thought up

Blackberry Eating

I love to go out in late September
among the fat, overripe, icy, black blackberries
to eat blackberries for breakfast,
the stalks very prickly, a penalty
they earn for knowing the black art
of blackberry-making; and as I stand among them
lifting the stalks to my mouth, the ripest berries
fall almost unbidden to my tongue,
as words sometimes do, certain peculiar words
like *strengths* or *squinched*,
many-lettered, one-syllabled lumps,
which I squeeze, squinch open, and splurge well
in the silent, startled, icy, black language
of blackberry-eating in late September.

Galway Kinnell

To a Poor Old Woman

munching a plum on
the street a paper bag
of them in her hand

They taste good to her
They taste good
to her. They taste
good to her

You can see it by
the way she gives herself
to the one half
sucked out in her hand

Comforted
a solace of ripe plums
seeming to fill the air
They taste good to her

William Carlos Williams

THERE
IS RAIN
IN ME

There Is Rain in Me

There is rain in me
running down, running down, trickling
away from memory.

There is ocean in me
swaying, swaying O, so deep
so fathomlessly black
and spurting suddenly up, snow-white, like snow-leopards rearing
high and clawing with rage at the cliffs of the soul
then disappearing back with a hiss
of eternal salt rage; angry is old ocean within a man.

D. H. Lawrence

why some people be mad at me sometimes

they ask me to remember
but they want me to remember
their memories
and i keep on remembering
mine

Lucille Clifton

Crying

Crying only a little bit
is no use. You must cry
until your pillow is soaked!
Then you can get up and laugh.
Then you can jump in the shower
and splash-splash-splash!
Then you can throw open your window
and, "Ha ha! ha ha!"
And if people say, "Hey,
what's going on up there?"
"Ha ha!" sing back. "Happiness
was hiding in the last tear!
I wept it! Ha ha!"

Galway Kinnell

A Strange Beautiful Woman

A strange beautiful woman
met me in the mirror
the other night.
Hey,
I said,
What you doing here?
She asked me
the same thing.

Marilyn Nelson

No Deposit

Sometimes
you feel
like
a
bottle
sitting
by itself;
no
return,
just
empty;
ready
to
be
thrown away.

Earle Thompson

I'm Nobody! Who are you?

I'm nobody! Who are you?
Are you nobody, too?
Then there 's a pair of us—don't tell!
They 'd banish us, you know.

How dreary to be somebody!
How public, like a frog
To tell your name the livelong day
To an admiring bog!

Emily Dickinson

Luck

Sometimes a crumb falls
From the tables of joy,
Sometimes a bone
Is flung.

To some people
Love is given,
To others
Only heaven.

Langston Hughes

People of Unrest

Stare from your pillow into the sun.
See the disk of light in shadows.
Watch day grow tall.
Cry with a loud voice after the sun.
Take his yellow arms and wrap them round your life.
Be glad to be washed in the sun.
Be glad to see.
People of unrest and sorrow
Stare from your pillow into the sun.

Margaret Walker

Patience

Patience wears my grandmother's filigree earrings. She bakes marvelous dark bread. She has beautiful hands. She carries great sacks of peace and purses filled with small treasures. You don't notice Patience right away in a crowd, but suddenly you see her all at once, and then she is so beautiful you wonder why you never saw her before.

J. Ruth Gendler

Oh Love

My love is a boat
floating
on the weather, the water.

She is a stone
at the bottom of the ocean.
She is the wind in the trees.

I hold her
in my hand
and cannot lift her,

can do nothing
without her. Oh love,
like nothing else on earth!

Robert Creeley

THEY
LOVED
PAPERCLIPS

They Loved Paperclips

They loved harmony they loved ant hills they loved food and cookies and harpoons they loved the sound of laces of the shoes and snow they loved the snow on Thursdays in the rain and when they met they loved that too and igloos and the trees and things to mail and chlorine and they loved the towels for the beach and hot dogs and the pool and also when the wind rose up they loved the ceiling and the tide and then they loved the sky.

Lisa Jarnot

The Red Wheelbarrow

so much depends
upon

a red wheel
barrow

glazed with rain
water

beside the white
chickens.

William Carlos Williams

Window

Night from a railroad car window
Is a great, dark, soft thing
Broken across with slashes of light.

Carl Sandburg

Skyscrapers

Do Skyscrapers ever grow tired
   Of holding themselves up high?
Do they ever shiver on frosty nights
   With their tops against the sky?
Do they feel lonely sometimes,
   Because they have grown so tall?
Do they ever wish they could just lie down
   And never get up at all?

Rachel Field

Count to Ten and We'll Be There

One chimpanzee.
Two crocodiles.
Three kings and a star make
Four . . . my new shoe size, just
Five days old. (I'm twice that now.) It's June—
Six more months until snow for sure.
Seven was lucky, not like
Eight, when I got glasses, better than
Nine, which felt Egyptian.

I'm ten now, which ends in
Zero. I've got
Four grandparents,
Three siblings,
Two parents and
One head with
Nothing to look at,
No place else to go.

Rita Dove

Today

Oh! kangaroos, sequins, chocolate sodas!
You really are beautiful! Pearls,
harmonicas, jujubes, aspirins! all
the stuff they've always talked about

still makes a poem a surprise!
These things are with us every day
even on beachheads and biers. They
do have meaning. They're strong as rocks.

Frank O'Hara

The Sun-Dial

Every day,
Every day,
Tell the hours
By their shadows,
By their shadows.

Adelaide Crapsey

The Bean Eaters

They eat beans mostly, this old yellow pair.
Dinner is a casual affair.
Plain chipware on a plain and creaking wood,
Tin flatware.

Two who are Mostly Good.
Two who have lived their day,
But keep on putting on their clothes
And putting things away.

And remembering . . .
Remembering, with twinklings and twinges,
As they lean over the beans in their rented back room that
     is full of beads and receipts and dolls and cloths,
     tobacco crumbs, vases and fringes.

Gwendolyn Brooks

Ways of Composing

typewriter:
a mouthful of teeth chattering
afraid to be quiet

a pencil can lie down and dream
dark and silver silences

Eve Merriam

Miracles

Why, who makes much of a miracle?
As to me I know of nothing else but miracles,
Whether I walk the streets of Manhattan,
Or dart my sight over the roofs of houses toward the sky,
Or wade with naked feet along the beach just in the edge of the
    water,
Or stand under trees in the woods,
Or talk by day with any one I love, or sleep in the bed at night with
    any one I love,
Or sit at table at dinner with the rest,
Or look at strangers opposite me riding in the car,
Or watch honey-bees busy around the hive of a summer forenoon,
Or animals feeding in the fields,
Or birds, or the wonderfulness of insects in the air,
Or the wonderfulness of the sundown, or of stars shining so quiet
    and bright,
Or the exquisite delicate thin curve of the new moon in spring;
These with the rest, one and all, are to me miracles,
The whole referring, yet each distinct and in its place.

To me every hour of the light and dark is a miracle,
Every cubic inch of space is a miracle,
Every square yard of the surface of the earth is spread with the
    same,
Every foot of the interior swarms with the same.

To me the sea is a continual miracle,
The fishes that swim—the rocks—the motion of the waves—the ships
    with men in them,
What stranger miracles are there?

Walt Whitman

THE GRANDPA KNEE

The Grandpa Knee

An old man who was old enough to be his own grandfather said to himself, Grandpa, may I sit on your knee?

And replied, Sit on your own knee, you're old enough to be your own grandpa.

But, grandpa, it's the grandchild who sits on the grandpa's knee.

Grandchild? Why, you're old enough to be your own grandpa.

But, grandpa. . . .

—But grandpa nothing! There's no sense to it, one grandpa sitting on another grandpa—It's redundant!

But grandpa. . . .

—If you don't stop grandpaing me I'll put you across my knee and give you a good spanking. . . .

Russell Edson

Note to Grandparents

the children are healthy
   the children are rosy
we take them to the park
   we take them to the playground

they swing on the swings
   the wind smacks their faces
they jump and are lively
   they eat everything

they sleep without crying
   they are very smart
each day they grow
   you would hardly know them

Grace Paley

Birth

When they were wild
When they were not yet human
When they could have been anything,
I was on the other side ready with milk to lure them,
And their father, too, each name a net in his hands.

Louise Erdrich

Metaphors

I'm a riddle in nine syllables,
An elephant, a ponderous house,
A melon strolling on two tendrils.
O red fruit, ivory, fine timbers!
This loaf's big with its yeasty rising.
Money's new-minted in this fat purse.
I'm a means, a stage, a cow in calf.
I've eaten a bag of green apples,
Boarded the train there's no getting off.

Sylvia Plath

The Little Girl

TSIMSHIAN LULLABY

The little girl will pick wild roses.
That is why she was born.

The little girl will dig wild rice with her fingers.
That is why she was born.

She will gather sap of pitch pine trees in the spring.
She will pick strawberries and blueberries.
That is why she was born.

She will pick soapberries and elderberries.
She will pick wild roses.
That is why she was born.

translated by Carl Cary
after Marius Barbeau

Dudley Wright

Lighting a candle for my father
I am also my father
lighting a candle

for *his*
in the past, where he is
also his father

lighting one for me

There Is No Word for Goodbye

Sokoya, I said, looking through
    the net of wrinkles into
    wise black pools
    of her eyes.

What do you say in Athabaskan
    when you leave each other?
    What is the word
    for goodbye?

A shade of feeling rippled
    the wind-tanned skin.
    Ah, nothing, she said,
    watching the river flash.

She looked at me close.
    We just say, Tlaa. That means,
    See you.
    We never leave each other.
    When does your mouth
    say goodbye to your heart?

She touched me light
    as a bluebell.
    You forget when you leave us;
    you're so small then.
    We don't use that word.

We always think you're coming back,
    but if you don't,
    we'll see you someplace else.
    You understand.
    There is no word for goodbye.

Sokoya—aunt (mother's sister)   Mary Tallmountain

Southern Mansion

Poplars are standing there still as death
and ghosts of dead men
meet their ladies walking
two by two beneath the shade
and standing on the marble steps.

There is a sound of music echoing
through the open door
and in the field there is
another sound tinkling in the cotton:
chains of bondmen dragging on the ground.

The years go back with an iron clank,
a hand is on the gate,
a dry leaf trembles on the wall.
Ghosts are walking.
They have broken roses down
and poplars stand there still as death.

Arna Bontemps

I Ask My Mother to Sing

She begins, and my grandmother joins her.
Mother and daughter sing like young girls.
If my father were alive, he would play
his accordion and sway like a boat.

I've never been in Peking, or the Summer Palace,
nor stood on the great Stone Boat to watch
the rain begin on Kuen Ming Lake, the picnickers
running away in the grass.

But I love to hear it sung;
how the waterlilies fill with rain until
they overturn, spilling water into water,
then rock back, and fill with more.

Both women have begun to cry.
But neither stops her song.

Li-Young Lee

While I Slept

While I slept, while I slept and the night grew colder
She would come to my room, stepping softly
And draw a blanket about my shoulder
While I slept.

While I slept, while I slept in the dark, still heat
She would come to my bedside, stepping coolly
And smooth the twisted, troubled sheet
While I slept.

Now she sleeps, sleeps under quiet rain
While nights grow warm or nights grow colder.
And I wake, and sleep, and wake again
While she sleeps.

Robert Francis

Acknowledgments

Thanks to the staff of the Academy of American Poets for all they do for poetry; to Tamar Brazis and Michael Jacobs at Abrams for making this book possible, and for making it well; to Ellen Brinks, Lee Ann Brown, and India Hixon for crucial advice; and to Melissa Ozawa for everything else.

Contents/Credits

HOW POETRY COMES TO ME

"How Poetry Comes to Me" by Gary Snyder. Copyright © 1992 by Gary Snyder. All rights reserved. Permission courtesy of the author.

"Sunday" by James Schuyler, from *Collected Poems*. Copyright © 1993 by James Schuyler. All rights reserved. Used by permission of Farrar, Straus & Giroux, LLC, www.fsgbooks.com.

"Substantial Planes" by A.R. Ammons, from *The Really Short Poems of A.R. Ammons*. Copyright © 1990 by A.R. Ammons. All rights reserved. Used by permission of W.W. Norton & Company, Inc.

"Eating Poetry" by Mark Strand, from *Selected Poems*. Copyright © 1979, 1980 by Mark Strand. All rights reserved. Used by permission of Alfred A. Knopf, a division of Random House, Inc.

"The First Book" by Rita Dove, from *On the Bus with Rosa Parks* by Rita Dove, published by W.W. Norton & Company. Copyright © 1999 by Rita Dove. All rights reserved. Reprinted by permission of the author.

"Permanently" by Kenneth Koch, from *The Collected Poems of Kenneth Koch*, published by Alfred A. Knopf, Inc. Copyright © 2006 by Kenneth Koch. All rights reserved. Reprinted by permission of the Kenneth Koch Literary Estate.

"Then and Now" by James Laughlin, from *Poems New and Selected*. Copyright © 1989 by James Laughlin. All rights reserved. Reprinted by permission of New Directions Publishing Corp.

"To P.J." by Sonia Sanchez. Copyright © 1969 by Sonia Sanchez. All rights reserved. Reprinted courtesy of the author.

"The Dog of Art" by Denise Levertov, from *Collected Earlier Poems*. Copyright © 1960, 1979 by Denise Levertov. All rights reserved. Reprinted by permission of New Directions Publishing Corp.

"Leaves of Grass" by Walt Whitman. Public domain.

THE SWEET EARTH

"Storm Ending" by Jean Toomer. Public domain.

"The Outlet" by Emily Dickinson. Public domain.

"The Pasture" by Robert Frost. Public domain.

"the detail" by Cid Corman, from *Sun Rock Man*. Copyright © 1970 by Cid Corman. All rights reserved. Reprinted by permission of New Directions Publishing Corp.

"maggie and milly and molly and may" by E.E. Cummings. Copyright © 1956, 1984, 1991 by the Trustees for the E.E. Cummings Trust. Copyright © 1973, 1983 by George James Firmage, from *Complete Poems: 1904-1962* by E. E. Cummings, edited by George J. Firmage. All rights reserved. Reprinted by permission of the Liveright Publishing Corporation.

"Solitude" by Charles Simic, from *Charles Simic: Selected Early Poems*. Copyright © 1999 by Charles Simic. All rights reserved. Reprinted with the permission of George Braziller, Inc.

"The Brave Man" by Wallace Stevens, from *The Collected Poems of Wallace Stevens* by Wallace Stevens. Copyright © renewed 1982 by Holly Stevens. All rights reserved. Used by permission of Alfred A. Knopf, a division of Random House, Inc.

"Fall" by David Ignatow. Copyright © 1991 by David Ignatow. All rights reserved. Permission courtesy of the Estate of David Ignatow.

"Revival" by Steve Crow, from *Mississippi Review*, vol 3, no. 2, 1974. Copyright © 1974 by Steve Crow. All rights reserved. Reprinted by permission of the author.

"The Waking" by Theodore Roethke, from *Collected Poems of Theodore Roethke* by Theodore Roethke. Copyright © 1953 by Theodore Roethke. All rights reserved. Used by permission of Doubleday, a division of Random House, Inc.

LOTS OF PLAY

"Lots of Play" by Gary Snyder. Copyright © 1986 by Gary Snyder. All rights reserved. Permission courtesy of the author.

"At the Playground" by William Stafford, from *The Way It Is: New and Selected Poems*. Copyright © 1977, 1998 by William Stafford and the Estate of William Stafford. All rights reserved. Reprinted with the permission of Graywolf Press, Minneapolis, www.graywolfpress.org.

"The Mind Dances" by Lawrence Ferlinghetti, from *A Far Rockaway of the Heart*. Copyright © 1997 by Lawrence Ferlinghetti. All rights reserved. Reprinted by permission of New Directions Publishing Corp.

Library of Congress Cataloging-in-Publication Data

Poem in your pocket for young poets / Academy of American Poets, Inc. ;
Bruno Navasky.
   p. cm.
  ISBN 978-0-8109-9142-2 (alk. paper)
  1. Children's poetry, American. I. Navasky, Bruno, 1967–
II. Academy of American Poets.
  PS586.3.P638 2010
  811'.00809282—dc22

                              2010023449

Trade edition ISBN: 978-0-8109-9142-2
Library edition ISBN: 978-0-8109-9882-7

Introduction copyright © 2011 Bruno Navasky
Compilation copyright © 2011 Harry N. Abrams
Book design by Liam Flanagan
Cover design by Maria T. Middleton

Printed and bound in China
10 9 8 7 6 5 4 3 2 1

Amulet Books are available at special discounts when purchased in quantity for premiums and
promotions as well as fundraising or educational use. Special editions can also be created to
specification. For details, contact specialmarkets@abramsbooks.com or the address below.

ABRAMS
THE ART OF BOOKS SINCE 1949
115 West 18th Street
New York, NY 10011
www.abramsbooks.com

Also Available:

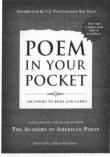

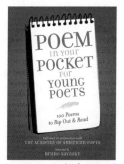

Poem in Your Pocket:
200 Poems to Read and Carry

Poem in Your Pocket for Young Poets:
100 Poems to Rip Out & Read